To: Ella
A magical story
for a magical you

From:

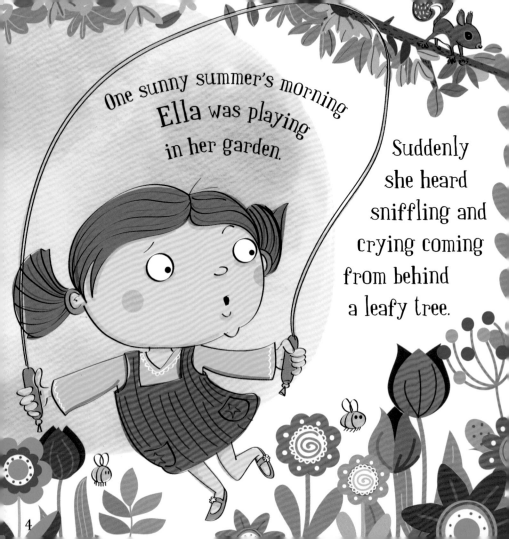

One sunny summer's morning Ella was playing in her garden.

Suddenly she heard sniffling and crying coming from behind a leafy tree.

4

Ella
tiptoed closer and closer
to the whimpering.

When she peeked around the tree
Ella was shocked to see a
little white and purple, sad-looking...

5

"Hello, my name is Ella,
what's your name and why are you
crying?" she asked the unicorn.

"I'm Sparkle, and I've lost all the magic colors on my rainbow horn from giving out **too many wishes**," said the unicorn.

"That's terrrrrible!" exclaimed Ella. "HOW can I help you get your magic back?"

8

"Well," said Sparkle, "as I become happier color returns to my horn and when I have all seven COLORS my magic powers are restored and I can give out wishes again."

9

Ella had a think, and a wonder and a ponder...

...what could she do?

"I've got it!" shrieked Ella.

"We need to do things that will bring back Sparkle's sparkle!"

10

#1

SO, they tried playing a game of hide-and-seek.

Sparkle wasn't very good at it but because she enjoyed the game so much the first rainbow color returned to her horn - ruby RED!

ching!

2

Then they sat on squishy
bean bags drinking hot chocolate
and eating rainbow-colored marshmallows.
This made Sparkle very happy!

slurrrrp

With a slurrrp of her hot chocolate,
brilliant ORANGE flashed up on her horn.

"I know what you need
now," said Ella...

"...a PAMPER day!"

So they wrapped up in fluffy robes, had their nails painted, and were so thoroughly pampered that sunny

#3

YELLOW

pinged back on to Sparkle's horn.

13

#4

Next up on their fun-filled mission was bouncing UP and down

doing somersaults on Ella's trampoline.

They were having so much fun that Sparkle's emerald GREEN band reappeared on her horn.

#5

Hungry from so much bouncing, the two friends went inside to make unicorn shaped cupcakes.

There was flour and eggs everywhere when the color sky BLUE appeared on Sparkle's horn.

There were only two more colors to go and Sparkle was feeling so much happier, but what could they do to get the last two?

15

"AHA!" exclaimed Ella, as she remembered the **fun fair** had just come to town!

#6

whizzed round and round and round on the last loop-the-loop Sparkle squeaked with such

They zipped up and down,

...a bright **INDIGO** band appeared!

elight...

There was just
one more
color to go.

17

7

Exhausted from all the fun
the two friends settled down to a
magical film and some **popcorn**.
Sparkle was **so** happy that
bold **VIOLET**, the very **last**
rainbow color, popped
back on to her horn.

"That's it! Thank you Ella!" laughed Sparkle. "You have made me so happy that **all** of my magical rainbow COLORS have reappeared and I can grant wishes again."

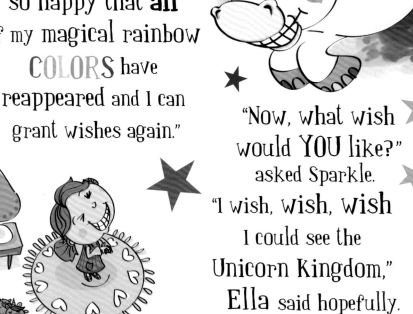

"Now, what wish would YOU like?" asked Sparkle. "I wish, wish, wish I could see the Unicorn Kingdom," Ella said hopefully.

With a
ZING and a ZAP,
a WHIZZ and a WHIRL,
Ella and Sparkle soared up,
up, up through the
wondrous rainbow.
Then in a flash
of twinkling pink light...

Ella couldn't **believe** her eyes,
she was **really** there and all because she
had helped a **unicorn** have **oodles** of **fun**!

The End

COLOR
ME IN